FUEL TO THE FIRE

CONNOR WHITELEY

No part of this book may be reproduced in any form or by any electronic or mechanical means. Including information storage, and retrieval systems, without written permission from the author except for the use of brief quotations in a book review.

This book is NOT legal, professional, medical, financial or any type of official advice.

Any questions about the book, rights licensing, or to contact the author, please email connorwhiteley@connorwhiteley.net

Copyright © 2024 CONNOR WHITELEY

All rights reserved.

DEDICATION
Thank you to all my readers without you I couldn't do what I love.

CHAPTER 1

A lot of people in the Great Human Empire might consider me a traitor, a monster and a murderer, but I actually don't believe that for a single second. There are a lot of things I would call myself because I am a hero, a bringer of truth and a destroyer of the corruption that worms and seeps its way into the very heart of all human planets.

That is why the Emperor created the Hydra Legion and that is why we betrayed him.

I, Captain Severus Luke, was standing on my massive oval bridge on the very top of my massive red blade-like warship, The Deceiver, because I was about to get new orders that would dictate my life for the next few weeks. I was rather excited to be honest. I might have to inspire an uprising, destroy a war effort or I might have to convince an entire planet that they were under attack when they were not.

None of that was hard to do and I really enjoyed my work. It was fun, freeing and I always had a good laugh whilst doing it.

My bridge itself was rather quiet today because I had sent off my normal command crew to grab an early lunch. I was glad to see them so happy considering the canteen had freshly teleported in meats, coffee and real fruit from a newly raided Empire world.

I was rather excited myself to be honest about the real fruit. I hadn't tasted the refreshing hint and watery flavour of actual watermelon for maybe twenty years. That was going to be an immense treat.

As my command crew were away for now there three tiers of bright blood-red holographic computers crackled, fizzed and popped as the ageing computer systems malfunctioned. Something that was starting to happen all too often through the so-called Traitor Legions.

But I always made sure to keep my ship completely sterile and clean because I liked watching my face and my surroundings through the shiny silver reflection of the floor. And I really did appreciate the sweet hints of watermelon, pineapple and grapefruit that all combined in a wonderful scent as the ship cleaned every single surface on the ship every so often.

A big flash outside the immense floor-to-ceiling windows that allowed me to admire the icy cold void of space and I was surprised that another Hydra Legion ship had arrived.

I smiled as I would have recognised that

particular red blade-like warship that looked as if it was floating peacefully in space anywhere. I had no idea why Cora Johnson, Second in Command of the entire legion was here alone but she was here and that was always interesting.

I didn't really know the last time she had travelled without the Legion Lord at her side. They normally burnt entire planets to the ground after us Hydra operatives had weakened and sowed more than enough chaos to make the planet easy pickings. It might have been a thousand or more years since she had travelled alone.

A blood-red hologram appeared next to me and I answered it. It was a voice-only message which was a shame because I always liked looking at the faces of my peers. It allowed me to judge them better and plan accordingly.

"Captain Severus," Cora Johnson said roughly like she was eating glass. "Permission to board your vessel the Legion Lord has need of you and your skills,"

I grinned. It was nice that my lies, deceptions and kills had managed to get back to the Legion Lord himself.

"Of course Lady Cora. I have entered it into the system so you may board whenever,"

"I'll teleport aboard immediately,"

I couldn't help but frown this time because I hated the idea that whatever Cora was sent here for was so busy, so important and probably so deadly that it couldn't wait until she had climbed up some stairs to see me. I also would have preferred to have my guards around me but that wasn't going to happen.

Tendrils of bright blue smoke swirled, twirled and whirled around the floor a few metres from me as Cora teleported in. I was surprised it was only her but as a superhuman myself I seriously knew the power of our presence.

A lot of the normal command crew hissed, coward and even screamed in my presence alone. I was three metres tall I suppose and that might be terrifying for a small baseline human, so I was glad none of them were in now with two superhumans present.

"Lady Cora," I said bowing slightly. "What tides do you bring about the war effort and from the Legion Lord himself?"

Cora smiled and that's when I noticed all the scars, slashes and cuts that covered her face as they twisted themselves into a foul grin.

"The war progresses like normal. The Empire burns, humans are slaughtered and taken to the mindcamps to become faithful drones for the Lord of War and the false words of the Hydra spreads,"

I clapped. That really was good news and once the Empire fell then it wouldn't be hard for the Lord of War to claim Earth and enslave the rest of the humans like he was always meant to. That truly would be a great day.

"Why did you need to see me my Lady?"

Cora crackled a little. "The Legion Lord has spotted a tasty world for us to take, corrupt and spread our beautiful lies. It is a Hive World that is a major recruitment world for the Empire Army,"

"If the world falls to us then the Empire Army will be weakened," I said knowing the drill and I was already so excited about getting back to work.

"But there is a major problem for us. Lord Commander Killian is already on the world and I trust you have history with him,"

I had no idea why I laughed but I did, because Lord Commander Killian might have been one of the best fighters I had ever met but he was loyal to the Emperor. That automatically made him an idiot to me but he was clever, skilful and cunning.

Even worse he was used to hunting down Hudra Operatives and being caught by a baseline human was a little embarrassing.

"By the Will of Hydra it shall be done," I said as Cora sent me the details and I couldn't deny the entire idea of burning a world inside out excited me a lot more than I ever wanted to admit.

CHAPTER 2

He never did realise until it was all too late that this mission was going to kill him, doom him and make him the most forgettable Empire war hero in history.

The choking smell of smoke, charred flesh and death filled the air as Lord Commander Killian stepped off his small silver blade-like shuttle that had picked him up straight from the spaceport, because the situation was so dire.

Killian dug his feet into the ash-covered ground and was almost surprised the ash completely covered his feet. He really wished he had grabbed a rebreather from the shuttle to help with the foul smell but he was a Lord Commander and he had to focus.

The sound of military boots kicking up the ash, troopers screaming out in pain and the crackling of flames in the distance made Killian really hate the traitors even more than normal. All around Killian were the burning remains of once tall, impressive and beautiful hab-blocks that housed thousands, if not tens of thousands of workers. Most of them were teachers, business owners and bankers that helped to make the entire planet a better-off place.

Petroleum 6 was meant to be a safe world that focused on petrol mining, recruiting troopers for the Empire Army and focusing on protecting the Empire. Killian had no idea how the hell a terrorist had ever managed to destroy so many hab-blocks so quickly.

All the endless amount of hab-blocks were twisted, collapsed, smashed up versions of themselves. They seemed like giant towers of steel and strength that were now corpses that needed to be avenged.

A lot of men and women rushed over in their green Empire Army uniforms but Killian didn't know what they hoped to achieve. They all looked the same to him and until Killian found a lead then they were all stuck with a terrorist out on the loose. And it wasn't exactly like this planet was short of hab-blocks to bomb.

Killian just watched as blade-like shuttles zoomed overhead as holo-grabbers reached down and started to pick up the debris. He already knew there would be no survivors but if the world wanted to believe that then Killian didn't want to kill their only hope.

Sometimes it was easier to believe in a false hope that helped people to stand up to fear, terrorism and murders, then to simply admit the truth. This was an unkind galaxy that wouldn't have battered a single eyelid if humanity was no longer in it. Killian almost shook with the realisation but he had fought too many wars, enemies and aliens not to know that simple truth.

And that was why he was a Lord Commander because he always wanted to protect humanity even in places like this when the terrorist seemed to only be a simple person and not an enemy force.

"Lord Commander," a very tall female said in the black armour of the Arbiters.

"Arbiter," Killian said bowing his head slightly even though it wasn't needed or correct at all. "What have you and your forces found?"

"The Terrorist died in the explosion so the case is solved for the most part. The bastard smuggled over two thousand litres of petrol into the hab-block, switched it out for the water system and lit up the water tanks," the Arbiter said.

Killian nodded. He hadn't realised the terrorist had been so clever, focused and cunning to do a plan that difficult without getting caught. He was even more impressed the Arbiters had discovered all of this within only six hours.

That was great considering the Arbiters' normal response times.

"Anything else?" Killian asked.

"Negative Lord Commander. My forces are withdrawing because we have concluded the terrorist was working alone and has no further attacks planned,"

Killian nodded but he could see something else was bothering her. He had only been on the world for about an hour so he wasn't aware of all the cultural nuances and what was really happening on the planet, but something clearly was.

"What's wrong?"

The Arbiter gestured Killian to come closer to her.

"Lord Commander this might be the worst terrorist incident in centuries but this isn't uncommon. Normally we stop the bastards but this isn't new for us,"

"What do you mean?"

"I mean," the Arbiter said looking around. "I have dealt with twenty attacks in the past Earth-week alone. Some of them are murders, some have been kidnappings and others have been terrorism bombings like this one,"

"Is there a pattern?" Killian asked hating what he was hearing.

"Negative," the Arbiter said. "There are no patterns in the environment, the background and the beliefs of the terrorists. For some reason an entire group of the population is deciding to rebel against Empire Rule and that means us Arbiters are very thin on the ground,"

"I think we have bigger problems than that," Killian said realising that if this world was on the verge of a full-scale rebellion against the peaceful, loving and protective Empire then there was a massive problem coming.

He had dealt with the damn Hydra Legion too many times not to realise that they would love this sort of so-called grand opportunity to spread their lies, deceit and chaos amongst the population.

"I need to take control of this planet immediately," Killian said.

"You have no idea," the Arbiter said. "The Planetary Governor will never allow it,"

Killian laughed. "Unless you take me to the planetary governor immediately then within a week this entire planet will be ash. Because the Hydra Legion are coming,"

"You mean… you mean the superhumans are coming?" the Arbiter asked.

"Yes and they will not stop until this entire planet is theirs and dead. Do you want to be taken to the mindcamps?"

"Please follow me Lord Commander," the woman said.

Killian just laughed as he followed because he was really excited about having a showdown with his old friend again. Captain Severus would be coming here and Killian fully intended to kill him this time.

He wouldn't escape again and Killian wouldn't allow him to claim victory here.

CHAPTER 3

I flat out couldn't believe how brilliant and exciting this job was as I stood on the massive oval bridge of the Deceiver with my entire command crew and my own Hydra Cell. I really liked how everyone had been kind enough to bring up their plates of delicious meats, refreshing watermelon and crispy smoky skin in their sandwiches. I was even better my own cell had been great enough to bring me up a watermelon.

I ate it in one which was a hell of a lot of fun.

As my command crew relaxed back and put up their feet on their holographic desks and my four superhuman Hydra Cell members stood in stony silence, I was really excited about briefing everyone for this mission. Not because it was easy but actually because this was going to be a very deadly, dangerous and uncertain mission that I wasn't sure I could win but as long as I had fun along the way then it didn't matter.

"Petroleum 6 is our new target," I said clicking my fingers so a massive red hologram of the planet revealed itself.

There were a lot of small blade-like warships zooming round the planet like bees around a hive but they didn't concern me for now. They would all be wiped out once the main battleforce arrived in a few weeks. Until then I was the only hope the traitors had of burning this world.

"I am familiar with this world," one of my Operatives said as he snapped a chicken bone like it was a twig. I had always liked Ryan, he was a cool guy that truly believed in the ways of the Hydra.

"True," I said. "This world is an Empire Hive World that is also a major recruiting world for the Empire Army. I cannot overstate the importance of capturing this world so we can starve the Empire of troopers, we can refill our own ranks and give the Mindcamps a lot more guests,"

I liked how everyone smiled and cheered around the bridge. It was certainly the way of the Hydra to enjoy the suffering of little baseline humans that were loyal to a stupid Emperor.

"The world will be hard to conquer for three main reasons," I said focusing on the hologram. "This a recruitment world so security is really tight, it is difficult at best and agents of the Inquisition will be everywhere,"

Everyone gasped and I didn't blame them. No one liked those idiots belonging to that all-powerful and top-secret organisation known as the Inquisition that had the power to burn the entire planet on a simple whim. They were that powerful and I just hated them.

If a single member of the Inquisition caught us then we needed to run like hell.

"Also," Ryan said stepping forward. "We have another problem with Commander Killian being on the planet,"

I was going to get to that bit next but I was sort of glad my Cell hadn't forgotten the distinctive golden appearance of Killian's Destroyer that was currently floating in orbit of the world.

"We can kill Killian easily enough. All we need is to simply get planetside first of all and that will not be hard," I said knowing we would simply be using standard Hydra procedures for landing.

A simple teleportation disguised as solar radiation would be easy enough.

"Then my intention is to start building up a network in the criminal underworld," I said, "and we need to find out who the hell is behind all the terrorist activity on the world,"

"Um," a large female said who was also a superhuman Angel of Death and Hope who was part of my cell called Flo. She was a hell of a warrior and she seriously knew how to convince anyone she wasn't lying.

"Something wrong?" I asked.

"The terrorism. It is clear this world wants

independence from the Empire but it is weird how there are no patterns," Flo said.

"Could there simply be another reason for the violence? Multiple cells working independently to achieve the same aim?" Ryan asked.

I nodded because that was a brilliant idea and one of my jobs when I got planetside was to simply get these cells to work together. And if anyone had a problem with me being a traitor superhuman then I would kill them just like I had done to plenty of other idiots over the centuries.

I looked at my last two Operatives in their crimson red superhuman armour. "Sonia, Freddrick any idea,"

Sonia grinned as she held her machine gun extra tight like she wanted nothing more than to simply unleash it against the Empire right now. I really did love that woman.

"Negative," Freddrick said already running extra scans of the world.

I couldn't deny that I didn't have an amazing team around me that all had their own specialty. Like Ryan was a great shooter and Flo was a great thinker and I was just a brilliant leader if I said so myself.

"Prepare to jump," I said looking out into the icy coldness of the void. "Remain cloaked at all times and let's get to our target destination. Hail the Hydra!"

"Hail The Hydra!" everyone else shouted.

Then space disappeared from view as we jumped towards our destination and I seriously enjoyed how my four stomachs filled with butterflies at the very idea I was going to see Killian again.

And finally kill him.

CHAPTER 4

Killian really didn't like anything about the planetary governor of the planet. As far as he was concerned the man was lazy, awful and just an absolute waste of space when his planet was literally burning all around him.

Killian went up a long wide white marble corridor with some of the most beautiful arcs he had even seen in the entire Empire, they were handcrafted and had some stunning little figures of battles carved into the stone. It wasn't very practical but Killian liked how it added such depth and texture to the corridor.

Up ahead there was an even larger white marble arc with some gold highlights that led out onto an immense balcony area. He could already hear the laughter, talking and singing of patrons as they enjoyed themselves all whilst the planet plotted to destroy them.

Killian hated (not that he ever would have told

someone) that because the Great Human Empire was so immense and spanned across more solar systems than Killian knew existed. All the different planetary governors were left to their own devices most of the time, because as long as they followed Empire law, paid their taxes and nothing too bad reached the halls of the Empire Palace on Earth then no one cared how a Governor ruled.

It wasn't even like 99% of the Empire had any form of democracy not that it was encouraged in the first place.

Killian smiled as he went out onto the balcony and everyone just stopped exactly what they were doing for exactly five seconds before they went back to whatever pointless conversations they were having about their day and affairs.

Immense light green bushes with red, purple and blue flowers climbed up the walls of the palace around the edges of the balcony area, and Killian couldn't deny the sight was stunning. It was why he loved the Empire and why he was always going to protect it no matter what.

The bushes were almost as beautiful as the stunning view of the planet below them. Killian loved how the rich dense forest below the palace looked so peaceful and calm despite the terrorist attacks happening and the cities in the distance looked peaceful.

It was all a lie of course but Killian appreciated a good lie. It was why he liked hunting down the Hydra

Legion so much.

The tall arbiter next to him frowned and Killian could basically feel her anger at being here radiate from her, but Killian needed an official escort and she would do perfectly. Not that it mattered because if the governor didn't do what he wanted then Killian would simply pull rank.

And he just hoped beyond hope the superhumans weren't here already.

The sweet aromas of fruits, spices and coffee filled his senses as a cute female waiter went pass holding a silver tray of fruit for the patrons to enjoy. Killian spotted the governor in all his golden, silver and copper robes as he went over to him and stuffed his fat face full.

"Governor," Killian said as he went over and he noticed how everyone was subtly staring at him.

He wasn't surprised that no one trusted him but these stares were different. It was almost like they were analysing and seeing if he was actually a threat or not. But a threat to what, that was concerning Killian more than he wanted to admit. A threat to the governor or a threat to their plans?

"What?" the Governor asked. "Can you not see I am having a party to celebrate the destruction of the hab-blocks? It was a wonderful piece of city planning but I am sorry the Arbiters couldn't get notified in time,"

Killian looked at the Arbiter next to him. She didn't even blink and now Killian was really curious about what the hell was happening on this world. It was clear that the governor wasn't fit to rule and if he was willing to bomb thousands of his own people then that was a crime.

So why were the Arbiters doing anything?

"Why did you bomb your people?" Killian asked realising everyone was looking at him.

"Because they were the scum of this planet. They might have been teachers, business owners and whatnot but I needed to build more factories and the blocks were in my way,"

Killian laughed. At least that explained why none of the systems detected the change of water to petrol and why no one had tried to stop it. It was all because that bombing was government-sanctioned.

"And why didn't the Arbiters do anything?"

The woman frowned. "I don't know. We follow our orders and we don't question the gov,"

Killian whipped out his pistol and shot the governor in the head. Everyone looked like they wanted to have a go at him but Killian just shook his head.

"By the Power invested in me by the Emperor of Humanity as Lord Commander I am hereby requisitioning this entire planet in preparation of the upcoming attack and I seek to guide this planet back to the righteous path that the Emperor laid out for humanity,"

Killian liked how everyone was nodding at him and he was a little pleased that only a member of the

Inquisition could actually question his position now. He just hoped there wasn't one about.

"What are your orders?" the woman asked.

"What is your name for starters before I name you Head Arbiter?"

"Layla," the woman said.

"Well Layla, get me all the information you simply can about these terrorists and bring them to my office. And get the Head of the Planetary Defence Force too,"

Killian looked up at the sky and he just wondered if Captain Severus was looking down at him or maybe even through a sniper rifle.

"Do you think they're already here?"

"Maybe," Killian said hating how his stomach was twisting into a painful knot. "Let's just get cracking. I fear we're already out of time,"

FUEL TO THE FIRE

CHAPTER 5

As the rich blue smoke of the teleportation swirled, whirled and twirled around me a final time before it all went away, I was so glad to finally be on firm ground once more. The plan had worked perfectly and the Empire was way too busy focusing on protecting their equipment from a major solar flare than us teleporting down here.

Of course they wouldn't even bother checking if the damn solar flare was real, but was what I loved about humanity. It was stupid through and through.

When the smoke finally cleared, I grinned as I found myself with my Operatives in a narrow underground sewage network with immense steel tunnels, not a lot of sewage and a lot of different sounds in the distance. It was times like this that I liked being a superhuman because I could hear there were humans up ahead, they were laughing and plotting and there were little mice running around.

If I saw a little mouse then I was certainly going

to snack on it because teleporting did take up a lot of energy, not that superhumans needed to feast a lot anyway.

I wasn't much of a fan of the sheer smoothness of the tunnel because that only amplified sound but we were children of the Hydra so we would be fine and our helmet made sure no sound from talking could escape.

I opened an Operative-wide communication channel and my smile deepened when I saw everyone's evil faces looking at me.

"Captain," Freddrick said. "My scans demonstrate the most effective route to the humans is straight ahead that way. There are only ten humans so we can take them,"

I shook my head. "Remember the teachings of the Hydra. We must learn about this planet, what are its weaknesses and then most importantly how do we feast on its hate of the Emperor,"

"The humans seem to be important," Freddrick said.

"Then let me sing to them with the song of my machine gun," Sonia said. "And then we will feast on their brains to learn what they know,"

"I prefer simply talking to them," I said, and I started leading us upwards toward were I heard the voices.

As much as I tried to make sure my feet didn't make too much noise in the sewage water, I was a superhuman after all so that was impossible.

I tapped into every single possible communication channel as I went and I realised that there was a lot of terrorist chatter. Every citizen of the planet was talking about it, everyone was scared and I could just smell the fear in the air.

This was a perfect world for my lies, deceit and chaos to spread. Whoever was the wonderful person that had decided to sow the fields for my arrival was amazing and now all I needed to do was make sure that the lies came to fruition.

And the uprising began.

"Just up ahead now," Freddrick said. "Two men. Eight women. Three women are wearing gold medals of a homemade nature. Not Empire in nature at all,"

I really hoped these were the rebels or terrorists that I had heard so much about.

Before we stormed out at the end of the tunnel I stopped and looked round the corner, there were three larger tunnels that entered the large square steel chamber the humans were in. There were no ladders, no signs of escape and no sign of weapons.

I was sure I could take them.

I went round the corner.

The humans screamed.

They jumped.

They whipped out knives.

They charged.

But I didn't even move as six of the women and the two men simply charged at me and swung their knives. As soon as their pathetic knives hit my armour they shattered.

"Sing to them Sonia," I said.

Sonia gave a crackling cry of laughter as she fired her machine gun and her bullets sang as they ripped through the air towards the stupid humans.

The bullets ripped into their flesh easily enough and I enjoyed watching the rivers of blood flow into the sewage water. It was good to know that the blood was going to have some use after all but I was more interested in why the two women with medals didn't attack me.

"So you are the Angels of Death and Hope? You must be the traitors but forgive me Lord I do not know the colour and names of the Legions," one woman said before I realised she was blind and her bones were too fragile to move or shake my hand even though she was extending her own.

"My mother," the youngest of the two women said, "is a massive supportive of the Lord of War and the traitor legions. Sometimes enslavement to good Masters is better than the freedom of dumb people,"

I forced myself not to laugh because she had basically just uttered a great deception piece I wrote a few centuries ago. It was always nice to see my lies lived on and influenced the minds of weak humans.

"Of course," I said. "Now I must tell you that your wants and desires have been answered because the Lord of War wants to free your world from the corruption of the Empire,"

"Excellent, excellent," the mother said. "This is

most excellent news. I told you if I kept inspiring others to commit suicide bombings then the Lord of War would come,"

I was getting more and more impressed with this remarkable woman by the moment.

"Is there anywhere we can get information please on the situation of the planet and I keep hearing something about rebel cells?"

The daughter smiled. "Of course my Lord. Please come with me and we will take you to the others,"

"The others?" Flo asked. "I did not think there would be a lot of cells working on the planet,"

I nodded. "Never understand the power of hating the Emperor. And as the Hydra wills it, Petroleum 6 shall fall to us,"

I was so excited that I was about to meet a whole group of humans that hated the Emperor as much as I did. This was going to be so much fun and I hadn't even fired my gun yet.

CHAPTER 6

Killian had no idea at all how that dumb planetary governor had actually stayed in power for so damn long. Killian supposed that his office could have been a great place but it was just so dirty, filled with rubbish and deadly that Killian just hated the place.

The office itself was a wonderful domed chamber carved out of the same white marble that Killian had really liked earlier. He liked how this office also had great little additions to the marble pillars that held up the golden dome at the top. There were things like dragons, monsters and beasts carved into the walls too.

The office could have looked amazing.

But Killian just hated how the silver stone floor of the office was chipped, cracked and there were so many stains on it that Killian really didn't want to know what he was standing in. There were probably some signs of drugs, alcohol and a whole bunch more of illegal things.

Killian coughed a few times as he tried to go through the mountain of dataslates and holographic reports on the governor's desk. They weren't organised, they were not in a pile and Killian couldn't make heads of tails of them so he simply gave up.

He couldn't believe that this was happening. He wasn't stupid enough to believe that every single planet in the Empire believed in the Emperor as much as him but he expected them to listen to the basic requirements. Governors needed to be organised, they needed to protect their civilians and they needed to always be weary of a possible attack.

It wasn't hard.

But he had managed to double check the information about the Planetary Defence Force going back years and years. It seemed that the governor had basically been killed off the force over the past decade. This planet should have had a force of over two hundred thousand but right now it was only a thousand strong.

It was pathetic.

"Lord Commander," Layla said as she came in with a large black dataslate. "This is the information you requested but I believe it might be quicker if I tell you it myself,"

Killian nodded. He just wanted answers at this point.

"Ever since the Former Governor had the Leader of the Social Workers Union assassinated.

There have been terrorist plots brewing constantly and at first there was a single movement called The Freedom Union and this was behind a lot of the attacks,"

Killian smiled because this was starting to make sense.

"The point of the Union was to overthrow the Governor and start ruling on there own in the name of the Emperor," Layla said. "The problem was that six months ago the Union broke away for a reason we do not understand and even worse the Union is dead,"

"Okay,"

"Now there are over two thousand cells and rebel groups working across the entire planet to overthrow the Governor and get their own people in charge. They have killed over two million people and the Governor never wanted us to deal with them,"

Killian was so glad the damn idiot was dead but now he sadly had to clean up his mess. The problem with a Hydra Legion operation was that the Hydra Operatives focused their lies, deceit and chaos on any grief that already existed in a society. They wanted to make people angry so they eventually rose up and focused on destroying their so-called oppressors.

"This changes now," Killian said. "Get me a Press Conference immediately and I need to contact all the major heads of the important cells. Maybe I can stop this if I get them to surrender and make them an important part of my government,"

"What?" Layla asked. "You're going to give terrorists a place in power. What message does that send to all the other planets in the Empire?"

"It will tell them then I am fair and I would rather focus our resources on the real terrorists and enemies. Almost all these workers want are innocent people that want to be treated fairly. I get them and I want to help them by showing I will not firebomb hab-blocks,"

Layla nodded and she went off to start on that. Killian knew he was taking a hell of a risk but he had to starve the Hydra Legion of any source of strength they normally feed from. If he couldn't deal with the fear, anger and want for change directly and quickly, Killian at least wanted to give the people of this planet a little bit of hope.

A moment later a very short little woman walked in wearing the black armour of the Planetary Defence Force.

"Lord Commander," she said.

"Get all available forces into orbit immediately. We need to make sure we can counter any threat that comes from the Hydra Legion forces,"

"Negative. I will not waste my forces on an orbital attack that will not come. My forces are better spent on the ground fighting terrorists,"

Killian shook his head. No one was making this damn easy for him.

"All due respect," Killian said, "I have fought the Hydra Legion before and they are coming here. They will kill us all if we don't focus,"

The woman laughed. "And all due respect *Lord* Commander you have never been on this planet before and considering you have just murdered my father in cold blood. I will not be following your commands,"

"Is that your final decision?" Killian asked not wanting to deliver the Emperor's judgement.

"I will not argue about this with the likes of you,"

Killian whipped out his pistol and shot her in the head.

"Then talk to my bullets," Killian said shaking his head and then he realised how badly he was shaking. He was glad no one else was here to see him fearful of what was to come.

He had lost more planets and millions more men and women to the Hydra Legion than he cared to admit. He simply wanted to be prepared this time and he just wanted to kill Severus.

But now he wasn't sure if he could maintain his humanity in the process.

CHAPTER 7

The Hydra teaches us that lies, deception and chaos are the fundamental truths of human life because humanity does not care about truths, they only care about emotion. Regardless of how bad and evil that emotion is, that's why me and my peers are so effective at what we do and why we can transform even the most important and loyal worlds into husks of their former selves.

As me and the other members of my Operative Cell followed the Mother and Daughter into a massive masonry chamber with immense brown stone blocks making up the impressively long walls, I couldn't help but smile. This was a great lair to conduct business from and it showed how great these rebel cells were at working to bring the Empire crashing down around them.

White candle wax rained upon anyone standing at the very edges of the chamber because I noticed there were tons of little candles lined up on wooden planks on the ceiling. It provided a lot more light than I would have imagined but then again, superhumans hardly need such silly things. It is our superhuman eyesight that gives us our strength.

I laughed inside my helmet at the sheer amount of human females and males in dirty brown, red and grey robes as they gasped at our presence. They all broke out into whispers and coughed and laughed that the Empire was finally going to fall.

That was an excellent part of the plan that was falling together.

"Private channel established," my helmet said.

"These humans seem right for the pickings," Flo said. "Look at all their focus, their smiles and their hunger. It will not be hard to make them work together and swear loyalty to the Hydra,"

I nodded because she was right as always, it was why she was the thinker of the group. The faces of men and women might have been dirty as hell but I could see the fire in their eyes and their rage at the Empire.

A rage that should have been easy to light up.

I followed the Mother and Daughter to the head of the large wooden table and everyone fell silent as the Mother started talking.

"Our sacrifices have been answered by the Lord of War himself. The Emperor might have turned his back on this world but the Lord has not. He has gifted us his Angels of Death and Hope and that means it is time to enact The Last Wall Protocol,"

I ran the reference through all the electronic signals I could hack into but I couldn't find any reference to this thing. And that concerned me.

"The Protocol will not work at this moment in time," Flo said stepping forward.

I smiled because it was times like this why I always made sure our Thinker was loyal to me.

"The Last Wall Protocol is probably some kind of attack plan or something to make sure the Empire collapses. The Empire's grip is still too strong on this corpse world and you know it. Do not allow your own biases to cloud your judgement," Flo said.

"What Legion are they High Priestess?" a man asked from the back.

I rolled my eyes. As much as I hated religion as much as the next Angel (loyal or traitor), unlike the Empire us so-called traitors knew exactly how to weaponise religion to make humans a lot more compliant with our orders.

"We are from the Hydra Legion," I said. "And the Hydra teaches us that the lies and deceit of this world must be exposed. Me and my team will start working on such news and propaganda. The Empire falls in short order,"

I was expecting everyone to start cheering, jumping up and down and screaming in sheer joy but they were not. They were more curious than anything else and now I realised I had made a massive miscalculation.

I contacted Flo and the others on a private

channel. "These are all working together already,"

"Impossible," Freddrick said. "My scans and calculations have detected six signs that they hate each other,"

"Maybe this is not an easy alliance Brother Freddrick," Flo said mockingly. "But the loyalty seems to be all about the Mother or the High Priestess as they call her. The orders must come from her,"

I nodded. "High Priestess we would like permission to do whatever must be done to ensure victory for the rebels and bring about the end of Empire Rule on this world,"

"You need not ask permission my Lord," the Mother said. "This act and this intervention on your part has been sanctioned by the divine Lord of War himself. And so I decree the words of the Angels are the same as my words,"

Everyone stood up and bowed and I just laughed inside my helmet. Humans were always so predictable in the end and that was partly why I loved my job so much. I loved travelling the Empire seeing what stupidity all the various human cultures could develop.

And each human culture only seemed to be getting more and more stupid as time went on.

"High Priestess," a woman shouted as she came into the chamber. "The Governor is dead. Killed by the Divine servants of the Emperor and now he is arranging a press conference and he has offered peace to the rebels,"

I hated how the damn rebel leaders around the table smiled, grinned and I could see they were actually happy about such an action.

"Come with me if you want to get to the conference," the woman said.

I was even more outraged that 90% of the damn room actually got up and followed them. That was a major problem because that meant all those people who knew exactly how many Hydra Operatives were here, where we were and most importantly who I was were now walking free.

They could turn against me and that meant me and my team had some framing to do. We had to kill all these weak rebels, make them believe the Empire did it and then we had to make sure they were only loyal to us.

That meant killing their precious High Priestess.

And I was so excited because then the lies, chaos and deceit could finally flow free.

CHAPTER 8

Killian seriously couldn't believe what the hell was happening with the planet. The south of the world was in chaos because of rallies, protests and murders and the north was tense as hell. It was even worse that the Planetary Defence Force simply wasn't responding to his orders ever since he had given their former leader the Emperor's Judgement.

He couldn't believe how stupid all of the people on this world were being because he just knew the damn Hydra legion were on the planet. That meant an even larger battle force was currently heading towards the world and soon there would be a hell of a fight.

And it seemed that only Killian wanted to be ready for it. He hated this world, the Hydra Legion and he was going to deny the enemy victory at any cost.

Hence the press conference.

Killian stood on top of a large holographic podium in the middle of a huge cobblestone square with little red and orange shops lining the edges of the square. There were a lot of blade-like shuttles and warships and transport ships flying overhead and Killian definitely would have preferred them to have landed but he couldn't issue a travel embargo now.

He simply didn't have the time.

Killian wasn't sure how many people he had been expecting but there were easily ten thousand people cramped into the square like sardines. He was glad he wasn't down there with them.

Some men and women in grey robes pushed and hit each other because of the sheer heat down there. Killian didn't care too much because he was glad to have the air-conditioning on the podium, it was the perk of leadership, not that any of these idiots ever had a real chance of achieving much.

"Today marks the day of a new chapter for this planet," Killian said, his voice booming over the square. "Today is a chance for us to move forward and start a better world for our future generations,"

He forced himself not to frown as he noticed a large group in front of him were looking like they were about to punch him.

"For too long this world has been unloved and that changes now. I will give full immunity for all rebel leaders if they simply desist their activities and join me. I will listen to them and make sure they are loved by the Empire,"

Killian forced out a smile to show everyone he was serious.

"Liar!" a woman shouted as she walked up on the stage.

Killian looked around for his snipers but he couldn't see them. That was hopefully good but he still would have preferred the comfort.

"This man is a liar," the woman said and everyone focused on her.

Killian recognised her as one of the most powerful business owners on the entire planet and she had spent millions on rebel activity ever since the death of the Social Workers politician.

"You all know me," the woman said, "you know I do good by you people. I have given my workers love, respect and plenty of good. When is the last time that ever happened?"

Killian carefully checked his pistol was still at his waist just in case he needed to kill her like everyone else.

"Never!" someone shouted from the crowd.

"Exactly," the woman said. "If you guys want me to become planetary governor then I swear to you we will return to the ways of our parents. That time when we didn't have to stress about food, water and basic medical supplies,"

Killian couldn't believe the sheer derangement of this woman. She had to be a Hydra operative, just had to be because this wasn't right. She wasn't normal, no rich person in the Empire wanted this to happen.

"Traitor," Killian said pulling the pistol on her and leaping off the podium.

Killian landed with a thud and he just knew she was a Hydra operative. They often used advanced technology to appear to be normal baseline humans instead of their superhuman bulk.

She was a traitor and she needed to die.

"If you pull that trigger then you will unleash a wave of death like you have never seen before. I am a Martyr," the woman said.

"Then you shall die as a Martyr to false Gods," Killian said pulling the trigger.

The woman's head exploded and the entire square went silent and Killian realised he had made a massive mistake and the Hydra Legion were working their evil tricks on him.

Killian didn't want to admit it but he knew he was too scared, too fearful and too nervous about the Hydra Legion. He had just killed an innocent woman and now the square was deadly silent.

The silence was broken by the scream of missiles.

"Oh shit," Killian said as the missiles lit up the sky and he teleported away leaving all his subjects to die.

CHAPTER 9

As the crystal clear blue sky turned a wonderful fiery red and orange and pink as the missiles roared towards the square, I had to admit that this was oddly working perfectly in my favour.

You see the Hydra Legion flat out don't get into the thick of the action until the battle force arrives, it simply is not the way of the Hydra. I rather like it but I will never deny the sheer joy of ending humans from time to time.

Anway, I was leaning on top of a local Government building made from wonderful white dirty marble that sent small pulses of warmth into my armour. It was rather great for a moment and I just focused on the beautiful sky.

I was using my superhuman helmet and vision to focus on what was happening down in the square, and it was seriously nice to see my old friend again.

Lord Commander Killian seemed to be alive, happy and up to his normal tricks. From what databases and personal emails I have hacked over the years, he always believed himself to be a hero, the stuff of legends and like after his death the Empire was going to make songs about him.

Of course in reality no one in the Empire liked him too much. They didn't like his fear, his nervousness and his sheer impulsivity that made him kill innocent people just because they *might* be a Hydra Operative.

I watched the woman's corpse just fall onto the stage and I was actually sad for her. She might have been useful in my plan, she might have had information for me and she might have been a powerful puppet for me to enjoy.

But she couldn't serve the Hydra anymore, not that she had in the first place.

The missiles screamed down and hammered into the square with such beautiful intensity that I laughed to myself. I knew the others were watching my visuals too so they would be smiling to themselves.

It turned out that the High Priestess had friends in the Planetary Defence Force so she had called them, told them to fire the missiles when I gave the command and they had done their job brilliantly.

And there always comes a time on these missions when I start to understand exactly what these baselines go through. And that was now. I appreciated that these people didn't really want to breakaway from the Empire, they simply wanted a leader that would respect them, love them and give them supplies.

At least when the battle force comes to take them off to the mindcamps they won't have to worry about those thoughts anymore. They'll barely be able to think what their name is, much less what their dry throat and roaring stomach means.

"Captain," Flo said in my helmet, "we have a problem with the propaganda,"

"What?"

"Freddrick here," he said, "the problem is that there are simply too many variables for me to run my calculations quickly enough. We need to choose our three main attack lines to rally the population,"

I watched as thick columns of smoke rose up into the sky and the choking aroma of charred flesh, dead people and burning rubber filled my superhuman senses. It was disgusting but it wasn't the end of the world.

"Interesting," I said. I always said that when my team came to me with a problem because I was their fearless leader after all.

"Boss," Sonia said. "Arbiters are breaking into the tunnels. They want to kill the High Priestess. Orders?"

"Let her die but kill everyone else. No Arbiters, no criminals, no nothing to challenge our versions of events. Let them die," I said.

"By the Will of Hydra," Sonnia said.

"Just let your instrument sing the song of murder and lies and let them die," I said and loved it when

Sonia laughed like a madwoman.

I frowned as I noticed there was a large group of Arbiters storming down the street below me. I was hardly trying to hide but this was bad.

If they looked up for a single moment they would have easily been able to see a massive three-metre tall superhuman in crimson red armour on a dirty white building.

"Ryan," I said, "I need you and your shooter skills at my location immediately. Kill the Arbiters,"

"Why don't you just flee?" Flo asked like that was the logical answer which it was.

"Because I have to see if there are survivors from the square," I said.

"En route,"

"You there!" an Arbiter shouted.

"Fuck this," I said leaping down to the street below.

The ten Arbiters screamed at me.

I whipped out my superhuman gun. I fired them.

My explosive rounds ripped into their flesh. Heads exploded. Chests shattered. Blood and brain matter painted the road.

"You okay boss?" Ryan said in my ear.

I nodded even though he couldn't see it. That was a close one but at least I now had a good idea about what propaganda to make that would really get the population of this world angry.

"The attack lines are Killian is a psychotic murderer, everyone who speaks out will be killed and everyone on this world is at risk of genocide. Work with that,"

"The High Priestess is dead," Sonia said.

"Excellent," I said descending back into the shadows because now my favourite part of the mission was coming up.

All because the grounds of this world were now seriously fertile so the lies, deceit and chaos could be unleashed.

And Killian could learn the consequences of his actions.

CHAPTER 10

Killian hated this entire world as he leant against the icy coldness of the marble balcony looking out over the forest below. It had been a week since the missile attacks and Killian really wasn't impressed with the state of the world.

The forest below him was blackened, charred and little fires were slowly spreading throughout. Killian had wanted to save this world so badly, he wanted humanity to live, survive and go back to serving the glorious Empire but the damn Hydra Legion had done their job perfectly.

He focused on the immense smashing and crackling and screaming that came from the distance as the immense city fell. Their buildings were collapsing, people were protesting and everyone wanted him out of office.

Killian simply shook his head. He had given this world everything he possibly could and all these humans were just so ungrateful for his guidance.

Killian had promised to open new water treatment plans, new hospitals and new farms so everyone could have fresh food and drinking water.

No one cared.

Killian had already had to stop conscription into the Planetary Defence Force because they were rebelling and he had no intention of giving rebels arms to use against him. And thousands of innocent people were already killed by these monsters.

"Lord Commander," Layla said as she marched in behind him. "I have the latest stack of reports for you,"

Killian laughed as he hated the foul aromas of smoke, charred flesh and charred iron that poured off Layla's body armour.

"Is there any point reading them?" Killian asked knowing they would only contain new details about new crimes, new uprisings and new criminal masterminds.

"Not really," Layla said coming over to leant against the railings next to him. "This world has got to pot because of you,"

Killian laughed. It was just so typical that he could be a military hero, he could kill thousands of aliens and traitors and still someone wouldn't care about his record. He was a hero to the Empire and no one gave a damn about the sacrifices he had made for humanity.

"Tell me Arbiter," Killian said, "have you ever seen your friends and loved ones and girlfriends killed in front of you? Their bodies ripped to shreds by superhumans. Their bodies dissolved in alien acid,"

"No,"

"Exactly, and yet everyone on this planet who has never seen the true horrors of war actually believes they can do a better job of leading this world than me,"

"You were not appointed by the Emperor or Regional Command," Layla said. "I have already written to them all and requested immediate aid dealing with you,"

Layla whipped out her gun. "I am an Arbiter, a law upon myself except for the Emperor and the Inquisition. You have broken more human rights and laws than I care to admit,"

Killian shook his head. She was such a stupid woman, so small-minded, so weak, so pathetic but that was the state of the Empire.

Killian looked at the burning city in the distance for a moment and he couldn't deny the urge to make sure that happened to everyone. What if the traitors and the loyalists could both die? What if he could deny the traitors the people for their mindcamps and stop the dying Empire from having more troopers for taxes and the Empire Army?

What if he could get revenge against the traitors that killed his friends and the Empire that didn't care about him anymore?

Killian laughed to himself. That was a great idea and it was a shame he hadn't seen this all sooner, plans would have to be made and he would have to annihilate this planet and return to his ship.

But that would be the best course of action. Deny everyone a victory and make sure both the traitors and Empire were closer to their own destruction.

Killian felt the cold barrel of the pistol against the back of his set. Such a stupid woman.

Killian spun around.

Punching Layla in the throat.

As she went down Killian grabbed the gun off her and he simply shot her in the head. The laser blast boiled her brain and her head popped but Killian didn't care.

He was so done with this world, these people and this Empire. If they were not intelligent enough to see that he was the best option and their only hope for the invasion then they didn't deserve to live.

But first Killian really wanted to lure out his old friend and make sure the Hydra Legion knew what he was doing.

Because he wanted to kill them all in the process.

CHAPTER 11

I was rather surprised when I stepped out into the sheer pitch-darkness of the narrow cobblestone streets of the main city what the hell had happened. Of course I had been monitoring the events all over the world intensely for the past week but like the teachings of the Hydra suggest. Lies spread without much force once the first lie has been spun.

In other words, it wasn't exactly hard to get the entire population angry, rageful and hateful towards the Empire.

Everyone had believed that they weren't safe, Killian was a psychotic murderer and no one was safe if they spoke up. That only made more and more people want to speak up.

It was even better when everyone, including the haters of the High Priestess, were so rageful at her murder (thank you Sonia) that they had all sworn loyalty to only me. I had contacted all the various rebel cells and terrorist organisations and got them to infect different branches of the Planetary Defence Force and the Arbiters.

Everyone was now loyal to me and I didn't doubt when the battle force came in a few days everything would be perfect for them. I had already ordered a lot of forces to withdraw because I still needed a planet for the battle force to invade.

I couldn't have it completely destroyed.

"Captain," Freddrick said in my ear. "We have a major problem,"

I rolled my eyes as I simply went down the long cobblestone street as the aromas of smoke and death and charred flesh filled my senses wonderfully.

"It is official Killian has just announced this planet is independent of the Empire,"

I laughed. "I guess that threw off your calculations easily enough,"

"You should hear him bitch about it," Flo said. "My Lord this is most strange and I cannot believe that Killian has finally cracked under our pressure but he must be aware his own death warrant has been signed,"

"Ran a scan of all transmissions leaving the planet in the past 48 hours. We might have missed something," I said hoping we hadn't.

"Here my dear," Sonia said. "Ten hours ago a transmission for Earth and Regional Command told them about Killian's inability to rule,"

"So someone wanted him removed from power using the official channels," I said knowing this person was already dead.

I turned a corner and waved as a small group of women waved at me like I was their best friend.

"If Killian is a traitor to the Empire and us then I do not know how to figure this into my calculations," Frederick said. "This simply adds too many variables,"

"Relax Brother," Flo said. "There is a logical solution and quite frankly there is only one course of action to take. Standard Empire Scorch Earth Protocol would likely be applied here,"

I hissed and turned down another street and grinned at the sheer amount of smashed-up buildings lining my path.

"I agree," I said. "Killian might not believe the Empire cares about him anymore and he would still hate us wonderful people. He is a blind fool that must be out of options,"

"Of course the Empire doesn't care about him. That is why I sing the song of death and murder and bloodshed to all the Empire fools that care to listen to my music,"

I really loved Sonia at times. She was crazy as fuck but I did love her.

"Captain," a woman said in the street to me.

I looked down at her and noticed she was wearing the signs of the Empire but she wasn't armed. She wasn't even scared and neither was I.

"The Lord Commander wished me to find you. He wants to meet with you because I believe he wants to destroy this planet. He has already scheduled a return to orbit," the woman said.

I snapped her neck as a thank you so at least she could have a painless death but that was interesting.

I had fought Killian many times over the decades and normally he was calm, calculating and so focused that he would never do something this extreme. But I had also met more than enough Empire Army generals over the years who had simply been broken by their responsibility.

Maybe this had finally happened to Killian.

"Killian is already at the spaceport," Flo said.

I shook my head. There were too many moving pieces, too many chaotic elements that were not in my control and there was a lot happening here that needed to be stopped. I know I was the leader but I needed time to think and I needed to consult the teachings of the Hydra.

"Contact the Battle Force," I said, "get them to arrive as soon as possible and prepare for immediate kidnappings of citizens. If we fail and the planet is destroyed I want to take some offerings to the Mindcamps,"

"Understood," Flo said.

"Ryan get on Killian's location immediately. If he tries to get on that shuttle kill him," I said.

"And me?" Sonia said.

"Start infiltrating a shuttle and get on a warship in orbit and start singing your song,"

"By the Will of the Hydra," Sonia said.

I shook my head because I needed to start separating my Operatives but I loved them all too much and this was a dangerous mission. I really didn't want anything to happen to them. They were all too important to me.

"Freddrick and Flo stay in the tunnels and prepare for extraction. I need constant updates about the situation," I said.

"Confirmed," Flo said. "What will you do?"

I laughed. "I'm going to meet with the bastard and make sure this planet remains intact so we have prisoners for the Mindcamps. Nothing else matters,"

"Shit," Flo said. "Incoming Empire battle force with Inquisitorial signals,"

And that scared me a lot more than I ever wanted to admit.

FUEL TO THE FIRE

CHAPTER 12

Killian went straight out to the little grey blade-like shuttle in the middle of the immense open hangar bay as three soldiers in black armour greeted him. He had already heard about the stupid Empire battle force and the entire situation was simple.

He had to get off this world and simply fire upon it. The Empire was simply stupid for not realising it was the only way to stop the Hydra Legion winning here, Captain Severus had to die.

It was that simple. There was no other choice.

Killian nodded his respects to the three soldiers as they took out a small holographic disc and the icy cold face of a female Inquisitor appeared.

"I am Inquisitor Nelson of the Emperor's Holy Inquisition and your forces are firing upon us. Tell them to desist immediately or prepare to be declared traitors," she said.

Killian just laughed. "Impossible. We are the saviours of this world. The Empire has turned their backs on me and these people. The Hydra Legion are running riot and I will simply burn this planet to the ground,"

"I hereby declare you traitor," the Inquisitor said. "There will be no chance of redemption for the like of you. I have a teleportation lock on you and then you will die,"

Killian whipped out his pistol and told the soldiers to cut the line. The Inquisitor was stupid because she was really willing to fight a true hero of the Empire.

The Empire was far more corrupt then Killian ever thought possible.

Tendrils of blue smoke appeared a few metres from him and he simply backed away. He could and would kill this monster because she was a threat to everything he valued.

Most importantly his life.

When the woman appeared Killian ordered his soldiers to fire at her endlessly and Killian was impressed with the tall superhuman-grade black armour of the woman.

But he had killed superhumans before. She was a baseline human so she would die too.

Killian shot at her.

Bullets screamed through the air.

The woman unleashed her machine gun.

Her bullets ripped into the soldiers.

Shattering their bodies. Their bodies fell to the ground.

Killian charged at her.

Leaping into the air.

He kicked her in the head.

She didn't react.

She whipped out a holographic sword.

Swinging at him.

Killian rolled backwards.

Again.

Again.

He leapt up.

Firing at her.

The bullet bounced off a shield.

The woman laughed.

Flew forward.

Leaping over her sword.

He punched her in the chest.

The shield flicked.

He noticed a dead soldier had a knife.

He rolled over to the corpse.

Picking up the knife.

The woman roared at him. She charged. She swung.

Killian rolled forward.

The blade sliced his shoulder.

He hissed in pain.

He charged at her.

He rammed the knife into her chest plate.

She hissed.

She went to roll backwards but she couldn't.

Killian rolled over to the other two corpses. He

grabbed their knives.

The woman was distracted.

Killian ran forward.

She swung.

He ducked.

He cartwheeled over the floor.

He rammed a knife into her knee.

He rammed another knife into her neck.

The woman struggled to move.

Killian kicked her sword out her hand.

He grabbed it.

And as the woman tried and tried to get the blades out of her armour Killian simply laughed and he chopped off both her arms. She screamed in agony and realised there really was no going back now.

He had already lost everything and everyone he had ever loved. It didn't matter if the Empire or the traitors had given his loved ones, friends and a chance of happiness away from him. The result was still the same so he simply smiled.

And rammed the sword into the woman's chest.

Then for good measure he chopped off her head as the cold distant dead eyes of the Inquisitor just stared back at him.

Killian looked at the shuttle and realised he didn't want something so dull and Empire-related to be his mode of transport. He grabbed the teleporter device off the Inquisitor's corpse and programmed his ship as the destination.

Bullets screamed towards him.

Killian leapt to one side. These were Superhuman bullets.

Someone with a sniper rifle was charging towards him.

Killian flew at them.

The rifle was too long for short distance.

Killian whipped out the holographic sword.

He swung it.

The superhuman ducked.

Killian grabbed the rifle.

Using the barrel to swing the superhuman.

The superhuman fell.

Killian smashed him over the head with the rifle.

The superhuman leapt up.

Killian swung the sword at him.

Slicing through the armour.

The superhuman punched. Kicked. Screamed.

Killian rolled backwards. Sidewards. Forward.

The superhuman was clueless.

Killian jumped into the air.

And even the superhuman didn't see what was happening as the sword was thrusted through his eyelids.

The foul monster of the Hydra Legion was dead and Killian couldn't believe how thrilled he was with himself. The Hydra Legion were here all along, he had proof and it just went to show how pathetic the Empire was.

They should have believed him and they should have trusted and protected him. But they didn't and now they were going to know the consequences of ignoring him because they were going to suffer.

And they were going to die for their stupidity.

"Killian!" Severus shouted as he roared into the hangar.

Killian activated the teleporter and simply went off to his ship. He no longer cared about Severus because when he was done with this planet Severus would certainly be dead.

And that was all that mattered.

CHAPTER 13

I charged at the bastard Killian only to see him teleport himself away in a twirl, swirl and whirl of blue smoke so I was left alone in the damn grey hangar with Ryan's lifeless corpse on the floor. I couldn't believe this had just happened.

Ryan was a brilliant shooter and sniper. He wasn't a specialist in hand-to-hand combat. He was a fool for going after Killian alone but he was a great person, a great friend and a great Son of the Hydra.

I went over to his corpse and carefully took off his helmet. His eyes were still open and they were staring at me. I closed them because I just couldn't focus on that cool, calm and wonderful face of his.

Then I took off the armour around my left hand and I grinned as I was about to perform something that a lot of loyalist superhumans thought of as dark, evil and twisted but I was a Son of the Hydra. The rules of man do not apply to us so easily.

I grinned as I pushed my fingers against Ryan's

skull but it cracked a little and then I dipped a finger into his brain matter.

Flashes of the battle, his thoughts and feelings echoed through my mind. I needed to find something that would help me defeat him but I couldn't.

Sure Killian had killed an Inquisitor but he hadn't revealed anything useful to Ryan before he died.

I went over to the dead Inquisitor woman as her corpse laid a few metres away. If a baseline human was here then I don't doubt for a moment they would have fallen over the woman's body but Ryan was a superhuman and Killian just wasn't normal.

I did the same again to get to the woman's memories and thoughts and feelings. She didn't tell me anything about the battle but moments before she teleported she was told a very interesting piece of information.

There was a structural weak point in the planet's surface caused by Empire activity on the world thousands of years ago. If someone hit that weak point on the north pole of the world then it would crack like an egg.

Killing everyone in the process.

I grinned because that was exactly the sort of information I wanted and I was willing to bet that if Empire records had shown that to the Inquisitor then Killian would have known that too.

That was how he was going to destroy the planet and rob the Empire of its soldiers and the traitors of its new recruits for the mindcamps.

Something I had to stop no matter the cost.

"Flo, Freddrick," I said replacing the armour around my hand.

"We're here boss," Freddrick said.

"Leave the tunnels immediately and get me a teleportation fix on Killian's flagship now. We have to change the plan,"

"Why?" Flo asked.

"Because if we don't Killian's going to kill us all in short order. Sonia is already on the flagship after boarding a shuttle. We have to help her and we cannot contact her in case it reveals she's onboard,"

"I think her singing will do that enough boss," Freddrick said.

I laughed because that was most probably true. Maybe the truest thing I had ever heard.

"I have the fix for you. Sending the coordinates now," Flo said.

"Excellent," I said. "Get on the flagship as soon as you can,"

"Captain!" Flo shouted. "Lost World Procedures have been activated by the Empire Strike Force,"

"For fuck sake," I said.

I hated how the own damn Empire was actually going to bomb their own planet into a wasteland to kill all the rebels. They probably believed the planet was too far gone to be saved.

But I was going to show them that no one steals a prize from the Hydra because if the Empire tried to cut down one of us. They were going to see just how many regrew.

"Abandon this world and get all the rebels to evacuate. Our Battle Force should be here soon and then we can collect our gifts for the Lord of War and the Mindcamps," I said.

"Hail the Hydra," Flo and Freddrick said as one.

But even I could hear it in their voice they didn't believe we could win here. And quite frankly neither did I.

CHAPTER 14

Killian flat out couldn't believe it as he teleported onto the massive oval bridge of his warship what was happening to him and his forces. The bridge used to be such a great place filled with happiness, delight and devotion towards the Empire.

There were always hymns and other important messages softly playing in the background but Killian realised that hadn't happened for ages.

He went over to the immense floor-to-ceiling windows and watched the Empire and his own fighters shoot each other, kill each other and just fight to the death.

This wasn't what was meant to be happening. The Empire was meant to see him as a hero but they were just foolish and blinded that this wasn't right anymore. And the Empire was going to learn the lesson and consequences of this foolishness.

"Lord Commander," a short woman said coming over to him.

Killian didn't even nod his respects to his friend.

"We have a situation. The Empire has given permission for a Lost World cleansing to happen," she said.

Killian just shook his head. If this didn't confirm everything he had ever thought about the Empire before then this simple act certainly did. They were meant to be the heroes and they were still going to kill an entire world because their calculations didn't believe it was worth their time to retake the world.

So they were going to burn it instead.

Then it hit Killian. He was no better than the people he claimed to hate, he was no less monstrous than them and now him and the Empire still had the same goal one way or another. This wasn't how things were meant to go out.

He was meant to be different. He was meant to be denying the Empire the troopers, not the Empire denying the troopers for themselves.

"What are your orders?" the woman asked.

"I don't know," Killian said, unsure for the first time in his entire life and military career.

"Captain!" a man shouted. "Hydra Legion operatives are teleporting onboard our ship,"

Killian shook his head. "Activate anti-teleportation shields,"

"Done,"

Killian laughed as he focused again on the immense floor-to-ceiling windows and noticed how there was a female Hydra corpse just floating there in the coldness of the void.

He still wanted Severus to be dead and then he realised that was what he wanted more than ever before. If he couldn't be different from the Empire about burning an entire world. Then he could certainly be different by finally being the person to kill the monstrous evil Captain Severus and his entire cell.

Cells were normally five superhumans strong so he had killed a man and now a woman. That only meant three left and he could deal with three superhumans.

"Get all forces to search this ship top to bottom. Find the superhumans and kill them. I have had it with these Hydra idiots and I want them dead," Killian said.

"Are you not going to lead the hunt?" the woman asked.

"No," Killian said. "For now let the Hydra run scared on my ship and let them know how much I hate them. Then when they're weakened they will know me as I shoot them all in the head,"

Killian just grinned as the woman walked off because he was finally going to get his revenge on the superhumans that had stolen everything from him.

CHAPTER 15

I slammed my fist against the cold grey metal walls of the corridor as me and Fredrick rematerialised onboard Killian's flagship. The corridor was awfully long, cold and it was nothing more than a straight line with a few metal pillars every few metres.

I hated that Flo had died.

One moment she was with us and then the next her teleportation signal had been cut off because damn Killian. She had been so bright, so intelligent and such a wonderful Daughter of the Hydra.

I had to find Killian and now I had to stop him. I couldn't deny the loss of the world was annoying as hell because we simply didn't have the numbers any more to stop the Empire and Killian from killing the world. And we had already launched our rebels into orbit and they were fleeing the world.

So on that front we were doing as great as we could and we were probably going to get victims but right now Killian was my target and focus.

I took out my superhuman gun and gestured Freddrick to start following me. All Empire warships were the same so it wasn't that difficult to find your way around them. The only problem was that the enemy knew that too.

"Sonia come in," I said inside my helmet.

There was nothing for a while until the sound of machine gun fire screamed into my ears.

"The enemy is listening to my song Captain. Are you onboard yet?"

"Confirmed. What is your position?" I asked.

"Boss," Freddrick said.

I spun around. Saw three soldiers.

I fired.

Bullets screamed through the air. Shattering the corpses within moments.

"By my calculations there will be more soldiers incoming in a few moments,"

I really didn't like his numbers at times.

"Captain I am nearing the main engine section of the warship. If I can destroy the engines then Killian is trapped and maybe…"

I nodded inside my helmet even though she couldn't see it. I understood what she was saying. If the engines were destroyed then the entire ship would be lifeless and Killian would be trapped.

But it would also mean a high chance of us all dying in the process. Especially with the Empire gunning for Killian and if Sonia made even a small mistake with the engines then they could explode.

Killing us all.

I kept going down the corridor with Freddrick close behind me.

"It's the only way," I said. "Sonia that's your mission. Destroy the engines and we all know what will probably happen. So make sure you sing a deafening Swan Song,"

"By the Will Of The Hydra. It's been an honour Captain," Sonia said cutting the line.

"This is going to pot," Freddrick said.

We turned around a corner and I noticed three different security cameras were looking at me. I shot them all but it annoyed me that the enemy were able to trace us so easily.

This wasn't normally a problem because the Hydra taught us that staying in the shadows was the best course of war and the best way to kill. That was the way to win wars.

But this wasn't a normal Hydra mission. We were going after a military target as basic superhuman assassins and this wasn't what the Hydra Legion was designed for.

I was going to have to adapt.

Bullets screamed towards us.

I leapt to one side.

I spun around.

Ten soldiers were storming towards us.

I fired.

My bullets exploded chests. Heads. Bodies.

The enemy screamed.

Their bullets slammed into my armour.

Echoing around my head.

I flew at them.

A bullet caught my kneecap. I didn't slow down.

I leapt into the air.

Landing on a human.

I snapped his neck.

I punched. Kicked. Killed all the soldiers.

"Captain!" Freddrick shouted.

I looked at him. He was firing endlessly.

Rocket launchers roared towards us.

I leapt to one side.

Freddrick screamed.

Three rockets slammed into him.

These humans were not kidding around.

I charged at the humans.

They didn't focus on me. They focused on Freddrick.

I screamed at the enemy. Their ears bled.

I fired.

I killed them.

I charged at them.

I tried to kill as many as I could.

All the enemy did was focus on Freddrick. He wasn't moving. Rocket after rocket pounded him.

When I had killed all the soldiers and stomped the rocket launchers under my feet I just screamed bloody murder at the stupidity of these baseline humans.

And I noticed that one of the dead humans was

wearing a cybernetic eye that was now flashing blue meaning someone was watching it. I knew that Killian was watching me and I wasn't playing his games anymore.

I stomped on the man's head to destroy the eye and then I gently tapped Freddrick on the back. I knew he was dead already judging by the twisted, sliced-up nature of the armour but I just wanted, needed to check that my friend was okay.

He wasn't.

I picked up his gun, knife and anything else that was useful on his corpse and then I went towards the bridge.

The time for mercy and being a Son of the Hydra was over. I was going to die on this mission I knew that but I was going to take Killian down with me.

Lies, deceit and chaos had gotten me this far so now I needed to use all my training to make sure Killian didn't escape this ship alive.

And that all started with Sonia.

CHAPTER 16

Sonia knew she was going to die after this task.

She had always served and lived by the divine musical teachings of the Hydra and she was more than willing to die by them in the interest of the Hydra. The Hydra always had to live on and in this case that meant destroying the engines.

Killian had to die.

Sonia slammed open the control panel to the engine room and stepped into the immense domed chamber with its black walls, huge iron engine chambers that contained the coolant and most importantly there was a large red holographic control panel in the middle.

Sonia carefully stalked forwards making sure she scanned the area with her machine gun as she went. There were no enemies in there for now and she couldn't understand it.

The entire ship knew they were here and that sooner or later someone would go after the engines.

It was basic tactical knowledge so it made no sense why everywhere was so unguarded.

The rich, thick smells of petrol, smoke and burnt ozone filled the air as she went into the engine room towards the holographic control panel.

That was one thing she had never really understood about the Empire holograms. It seemed that when someone was loyal they were always blue but when they were traitor they were another colour. It was weird. It was almost like warships of the Empire were self-aware and aware of their Masters' loyalties to the throne world.

Sonia managed to get to the control panel and she shook her head. She recognised a lot of these symbols and it was strange seeing them all so perfectly aligned almost like the control panel wanted her to touch it.

"I wouldn't do that if I was you Hydra scum," a man said.

Sonia turned around and laughed at the hulking three-metre-tall superhuman in fiery red armour. It was odd that a single member of the Ignis legion, one of the three loyal to the Emperor, would actually be here alone.

Sonia aimed her machine gun at him.

The warrior laughed. "I have killed my friends so I may serve Killian. If I am happy to do that to a friend then imagine what I will do to a foe,"

"Then you shall listen to the roar and song of the Hydra," Sonia said.

She fired.

The warrior charged.

He rolled to one side.

He flew at her.

He was quick. All superhuman reflexes and instincts.

Sonia kept firing.

The bullets slammed into him.

Slowing him down.

He whipped out his own gun.

Sonia aimed for the gun.

It exploded in the Warrior's hand.

The warrior charged at her.

Sonia rolled to one side.

The warrior punched at her.

She dodged.

He punched again. Again. Again.

He was too quick.

He kicked her.

Sonia fell backwards.

She landed with a thud.

The warrior went to jump on her.

Sonia rolled to one side.

The warrior landed.

Sonia leapt up.

Punching him in the helmet.

His helmet cracked.

The warrior whipped out a holographic sword.

He swung it.

It sliced through her armour.

Hitting flesh.

She screamed. Superhuman drugs and hormones flooded her body.

Sonia whipped up her machine gun. She fired.

A constant song and scream of bullets smashed into the warrior.

The warrior's armour buckled and cracked.

He flew at her.

Sonia's eyes widened.

The recoil stopped her from moving.

The warrior slammed the blade into her stomach.

Slicing through her armour.

Sonia gripped the warrior's wrist so he couldn't back away. She raised the machine gun to his chest.

And she fired until the weapon was empty.

The holographic blade deactivated and the warrior's corpse hit the ground with a thud.

She could hear the foul hammering footsteps of more enemy soldiers coming towards her but she didn't care. She knew she was going to die and that was okay.

She felt the warm droplets of blood pour down her stomach and legs more and more as she turned back to the control panel.

Sonia recognised the symbols a lot more now she didn't have to worry about an enemy ambushing her. She simply flicked, clicked and wiped some of the symbols together. All before she kicked the control panel so hard that it broke.

The engines screamed as the coolant bursted out

of the chambers and Sonia just laughed as the tidal wave of coolant rushed towards her. The wave would kill her even quicker.

But she had done her job, her duty and her service to the Hydra and Severus. And most importantly her machine gun had sung a final song and that was a life well-lived to Sonia.

Now everything rested on Severus.

CHAPTER 17

With two superhuman guns in my hand I marched up the massive spinal corridor of the warship. The corridor was exactly like most Empire warships with grey walls, a square design and a door or archway that led into another corridor every ten or twenty metres. But there were no enemies so far.

I was so glad that wonderful Sonia had done her job, her duty and she had always been a fine warrior in the memory of the Legion. I could already start to hear the humming, popping and vibrating of the ship from the engines starting to decrease and slow down.

Killian wasn't escaping and sooner or later the entire ship would simply become a sitting duck.

"Captain Severus," a man said over my communication network. "This is Commander Raven of the Hydra Legion. Battle Force is about to drop out of Slidespace now. Status?"

I grinned. This was amazing and I really did love my legion.

"Commander I am the only survivor of my cell. I am on Killian's flagship and am going to kill him. Empire has ordered a Lost World event on the planet and rebels and other people are in orbit. Get them,"

"Of course. Happy hunting," the Commander said as he cut the link.

I felt so much hope for a moment as I continued along the corridor because with the Battle Force here then it meant there was a chance I could escape, live and make sure the work of the Hydra never ended.

I went past a small holographic panel in the corridor and grinned as I activated it.

The key to the Ways of the Hydra was to simply make sure you never ever stopped deceiving, lying and causing chaos. So I simply entered a bunch of code into the computer systems that was a little old school for my liking but it did the trick as everything went to hell on the ship.

Warning sirens screamed all around the ship. Weapon systems stopped moving. And I heard tons of false readings about my location going through like wildfire.

And the cherry on top was that I could hear people leaving the bridge to simply go and check if I was there or not.

I checked my waist to see what I had picked up when I had searched Freddrick's corpse and I found a very small cloaker that he had probably made himself. He was always doing great things like that.

I stuck it on my armour and as the soldiers from

the bridge went past me I simply grinned as not a single one of them realised I was there.

It would have been so easy for me to kill them all but I couldn't do that. I had to draw them away from the bridge so I could kill Killian without him getting any extra support.

Once all the soldiers had gone past me and I didn't deactivate the cloaker I simply stalked towards the bridge in a light run.

I got to the massively thick steel door of the bridge, I clicked it and I went inside.

Killian was standing there smiling at me as I went in and deactivated the cloaker. The bridge wasn't that nice because it looked just like all the other Empire bridges with its oval shape, tiers of holographic computers and immense floor-to-ceiling windows.

Killian whipped out a pistol and a holographic blade that might have been malfunctioning because of how badly it was crackling.

"You took everything from me," Killian said.

"You did that to yourself," I said. "You did that when the Hydra won inside your mind. Admit it we broke you, we broke a war hero and now you have doomed an entire world because of your foolishness,"

Killian shook his head. "Never. I am a hero and it is everyone else that is the monster. You didn't break me because you gave me the clarity to see what needed to be done,"

"You really are deluded,"

"Well it seems delusions get results. Now tell me

Hydra Captain where are your friends? All dead yet? You can join them soon enough!"

He had no right to say that. I flew at him.

Aiming my guns. I fired.

The bullets screamed towards him.

He rolled to one side.

He was quick.

He charged at me.

I swung his sword.

I used a gun to parry it.

He just stared at me. "Your armour is stronger than I thought. But your death is still a certainty traitor,"

He roared. He flew at me.

I blocked again. Again.

He was too rapid.

His blade blurred.

He fired his pistols.

Popping off the armour around my kneecap.

I hissed in pain.

He kicked it.

He fired again.

Shooting me in the kneecap.

I collapsed to the ground.

Killian kicked me in the head.

I landed with a thud and then he jammed the icy cold barrel of the pistol against my head.

He was about to pull the trigger.

CHAPTER 18

Killian seriously flat out couldn't believe that this was finally going to happen as he pressed the cold barrel of his pistol against Severus's head. He was finally going to kill the monster that had stolen everything from him, Severus was going to die and he would never ever be a problem to the galaxy ever again.

That was going to be amazing.

Killian stared at Severus. He was so weak, so stupid and so foolish up close just like everyone else was because Killian was the smartest man that had ever existed.

"You have failed your Hydra," Killian said. "The traitor and the Empire will both die in the end and that is a good thing. The sooner the galaxy and humanity can be rid of them the better,"

Killian didn't understand why Severus laughed at him.

"The Hydra isn't something that can be killed. It

is an idea, a teaching and a book offering us hope against the stupid Emperor and it is guidance towards enslaving humanity so those that know better can rule it,"

Killian hated every single damn word that came out of this idiot's mouth.

"So you might kill me but the Hydra has one final lesson for me to use," Severus said.

"What?" Killian asked.

"Don't die lying down,"

Severus punched him.

Killian hissed in agony as he felt his jaw break.

Severus threw him off him.

Killian landed. He jumped back up.

He pointed his sword at Severus. He aimed his pistol. He fired.

The bullets screamed towards the superhuman but they bounced off his armour.

Killian aimed for the kneecap that made Severus limp a little but his pistol didn't fire.

Click went the trigger. Click. Click. Click.

Killian's eyes widened as he realised exactly what was happening. He never should have left the Empire. He never should have betrayed them. He should have continued to believe in the Emperor.

But that ship had well and truly died inside him.

Maybe if he was still loyal to the Empire and everything would have been okay and ended differently but he was too stupid, too desperate and too chaotic to simply allow himself to see that simple truth.

Severus didn't even charge at him.

Killian felt his arms become heavy and he allowed the empty pistol to simply slip out of his hands and it hit the floor hard. So hard he was sure if there had been any bullets left in it it would have fired.

He weakly raised his sword to defend against the superhuman monster walking towards him but Killian didn't want to fight anymore.

He was a traitor to the Empire he had sworn to love, serve and protect but he had failed.

"You seem defeated now," Severus said stopping around a metre from him.

"Maybe I am old friend," Killian said. "I chased you and your cell all over the Empire and I tried to stop you each and every time. I saw what you were doing, I saw how many lives you were destroying and still I couldn't do anything,"

"It is simply the Way of the Hydra,"

"Maybe, but you are right you did break me. I thought this was my chance to stop you and get ahead of you and your forces. Your tactics are perfect, I will admit but I thought since you weren't on the planet yet there was time for you to be stopped,"

"You cannot stop the march of the Hydra. Humans will always believe in lies, deceit and half more than truth,"

Killian nodded because he understood full of that now. It really was one of the foundational truths of the Empire and humanity as a whole and it was just annoying that it was the traitors had worked it out.

The very last people he had ever wanted to.

Severus took the holographic blade out of Killian's hands and Killian let him.

"What will happen to the humans?" Killian asked.

"Goodbye old friend," Severus said. "I have my own warship to escape to and you have Empire company behind you. Now you will face the consequences of your actions. I am almost just sad I do not have the honour of delivering the Emperor's Judgement to you,"

Killian was about to ask what he meant when Severus teleported away in a blue puff of smoke. It was a shame the damn engines had failed otherwise Severus would be trapped with him.

Killian turned around and frowned as he saw ten Empire blade-like bombers race towards him and his ship.

There was nothing else he could do because this was simply the way things had to be. He was a traitor, he had made a stupid decision out of fear and now he was going to die.

He supposed this wasn't the worst way to go because he got to die in a fight and he got to die knowing what he had done was flat out wrong. He couldn't be redeemed but he could get peace in death.

And dying in a battle was the best way for a

warrior to die.

"For the Emperor," Killian said as the bombs smashed down on his warship and shattered it like an egg.

CHAPTER 19

As I stood on the immense oval bridge of my warship, The Deceiver, I just grinned to myself. Because everything really was right with the world and especially on my warship. The crew were already celebrating in the mess and canteens stuffing their faces full of pies, ice cream and real fruit that we had been gifted yet again.

I might have been alone in the bridge with only the humming, banging and vibrating of the ship from the engines to keep me company that my team were all sadly dead, but that was actually the point of all of this. I was never truly alone.

The holographic computers that my command crew normally sat on might have been empty. The large hologram that was normally in the middle of the bridge might have been off, and I might have been waiting for Cora Johnson to contact me again.

But I was never alone.

I focused on the vast crimson fleet of blade-like

warships. I watched them dance and swirl and twirl in the cold void of space and I felt such a wave of happiness rush over me, because I was alive and I was part of this Legion.

My closest and dearest friends might have died but they died doing what the Hydra wanted them to do. They were fighting for the traitor legions, fighting to doom humanity and fighting to make sure the Emperor fell.

There really was no more honourable way for a Son or Daughter of the Hydra to die. and most importantly Killian was dead so he could never serve the Empire or kill another traitor ever again.

And that was what mattered most.

Small hints of watermelon, grapefruit and oranges started to fill the bridge, making the great taste of fruit salad form on my tongue. It was strange in a way because that was such a human reaction to the smell. Maybe I am a lot more human and relatable than I thought possible and maybe I am a far better person than Killian ever was.

Now that really would be a scary thought or realisation.

A small red hologram appeared by my hand and I smiled because this was the call I had been waiting for all day. Cora Johnstone actually looked good today in her crimson armour but it was difficult to tell if the armour had gotten a new paint job or something since the hologram itself was red too.

"Cora," I said smiling at one of the legion's most

important warriors but I didn't bow.

"Captain Severus," she said, her voice a little emotional for a change. "You have done excellently and the Legion Lord congratulates you, and please know the Hydra will remember your team,"

"Thank you," I said bowing my head slightly. "But why is there congratulations? I failed a mission parameter,"

Cora nodded in her red holographic form. "That is one way to look at it but the Hydra still supports you. You bought an entire world to collapse, you got us five million more humans for the mindcamps that will go to be loyal mindless soldiers in the fight against the Empire and now Lord Commander Killian is dead,"

"Could we have used him?" I asked.

Cora laughed. "Flipping a highly decorated Empire Lord Commander is not something the Hydra teaches. We flip weaker members of the Empire that is it. Relax Captain, you have done us a great service today. A service that will have consequences that will ring down the ages,"

I smiled because that was a lot of comfort and I was looking forward to developing a new team so we could go on missions, spread more chaos and help the Empire come one step closer towards its own damnation.

"Until we meet again Captain," Cora said. "Hail the Hydra,"

"Hail The Hydra," I said as the bridge went silent

and Cora's hologram disappeared.

I still couldn't believe how happy I felt because there were so many worlds, so many people and so many possible weaknesses of the Empire to exploit. And that meant there were a lot of fun, interesting and exciting times ahead for me.

And as my friends and command crew came back into the bridge with their hands full of watermelons, grapefruits and oranges I laughed because I really was living my best life surrounded by people that loved, cared and respected me.

The very best sort of people.

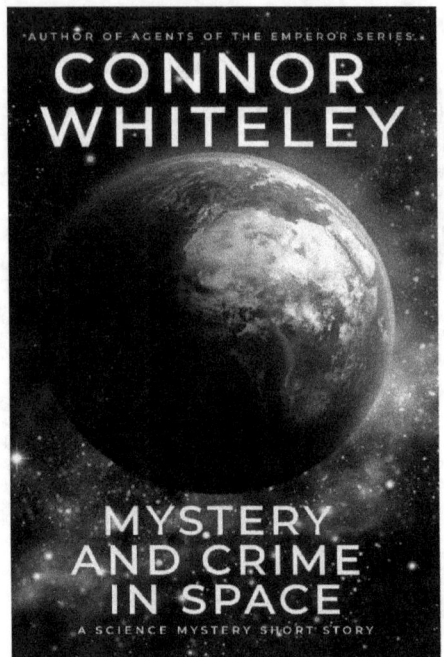

GET YOUR FREE SHORT STORY NOW!

And get signed up to Connor Whiteley's newsletter to hear about new gripping books, offers and exciting projects. (You'll never be sent spam)

https://www.subscribepage.io/garrosignup

About the author:

Connor Whiteley is the author of over 60 books in the sci-fi fantasy, nonfiction psychology and books for writer's genre and he is a Human Branding Speaker and Consultant.

He is a passionate warhammer 40,000 reader, psychology student and author.

Who narrates his own audiobooks and he hosts The Psychology World Podcast.

All whilst studying Psychology at the University of Kent, England.

Also, he was a former Explorer Scout where he gave a speech to the Maltese President in August 2018 and he attended Prince Charles' 70th Birthday Party at Buckingham Palace in May 2018.

Plus, he is a self-confessed coffee lover!

Other books by Connor Whiteley:

Bettie English Private Eye Series

A Very Private Woman

The Russian Case

A Very Urgent Matter

A Case Most Personal

Trains, Scots and Private Eyes

The Federation Protects

Cops, Robbers and Private Eyes

Just Ask Bettie English

An Inheritance To Die For

The Death of Graham Adams

Bearing Witness

The Twelve

The Wrong Body

The Assassination Of Bettie English

Wining And Dying

Eight Hours

Uniformed Cabal

A Case Most Christmas

Gay Romance Novellas

Breaking, Nursing, Repairing A Broken Heart

Jacob And Daniel

Fallen For A Lie

Spying And Weddings

Clean Break

Awakening Love
Meeting A Country Man
Loving Prime Minister
Snowed In Love
Never Been Kissed
Love Betrays You

<u>Lord of War Origin Trilogy:</u>
Not Scared Of The Dark
Madness
Burn Them All

<u>Way Of The Odyssey</u>
Odyssey of Rebirth
Convergence of Odysseys

<u>Lady Tano Fantasy Adventure Stories</u>
Betrayal
Murder
Annihilation

<u>The Fireheart Fantasy Series</u>
Heart of Fire
Heart of Lies
Heart of Prophecy
Heart of Bones
Heart of Fate

<u>City of Assassins (Urban Fantasy)</u>
City of Death
City of Martyrs
City of Pleasure
City of Power

<u>Agents of The Emperor</u>
Return of The Ancient Ones
Vigilance
Angels of Fire
Kingmaker
The Eight
The Lost Generation
Hunt
Emperor's Council
Speaker of Treachery
Birth Of The Empire
Terraforma
Spaceguard

<u>The Rising Augusta Fantasy Adventure Series</u>
Rise To Power
Rising Walls
Rising Force
Rising Realm

Lord Of War Trilogy (Agents of The Emperor)
Not Scared Of The Dark
Madness
Burn It All Down

Miscellaneous:
RETURN
FREEDOM
SALVATION
Reflection of Mount Flame
The Masked One
The Great Deer
English Independence

OTHER SHORT STORIES BY CONNOR WHITELEY

Mystery Short Story Collections
Criminally Good Stories Volume 1: 20 Detective Mystery Short Stories
Criminally Good Stories Volume 2: 20 Private Investigator Short Stories
Criminally Good Stories Volume 3: 20 Crime Fiction Short Stories
Criminally Good Stories Volume 4: 20 Science Fiction and Fantasy Mystery Short Stories

Criminally Good Stories Volume 5: 20 Romantic Suspense Short Stories

<u>Connor Whiteley Starter Collections:</u>
Agents of The Emperor Starter Collection
Bettie English Starter Collection
Matilda Plum Starter Collection
Gay Romance Starter Collection
Way Of The Odyssey Starter Collection
Kendra Detective Fiction Starter Collection

<u>Mystery Short Stories:</u>
Protecting The Woman She Hated
Finding A Royal Friend
Our Woman In Paris
Corrupt Driving
A Prime Assassination
Jubilee Thief
Jubilee, Terror, Celebrations
Negative Jubilation
Ghostly Jubilation
Killing For Womenkind
A Snowy Death
Miracle Of Death
A Spy In Rome
The 12:30 To St Pancreas
A Country In Trouble

A Smokey Way To Go
A Spicy Way To GO
A Marketing Way To Go
A Missing Way To Go
A Showering Way To Go
Poison In The Candy Cane
Kendra Detective Mystery Collection Volume 1
Kendra Detective Mystery Collection Volume 2
Mystery Short Story Collection Volume 1
Mystery Short Story Collection Volume 2
Criminal Performance
Candy Detectives
Key To Birth In The Past

www.ingramcontent.com/pod-product-compliance
Lightning Source LLC
LaVergne TN
LVHW012120070526
838202LV00056B/5806